Black bird, quack bird, riding on a back bird,

Puffed bird, stuffed bird, doesn't do a lot.

Hoot bird, fruit bird, whistles like a flute bird,

Toddle bird, Waddle bird, isn't that a model bird?

Jail bird,

snail bird,

showing off his tail bird,

splash bird,

crash bird,

landing with a BUMP!

SWOOP bird,

POOP bird,

flying **loop-the-loop** bird,

crown bird,

frown bird . . .

Cheer up,
GRUMP!

Jerky bird, turkey bird, strange and quirky bird,

clock bird, CUCKOO!

croc bird, cleaning up a mouth.

King bird,

sing bird,

sleeping on the **Wing** bird,

deliver bird,

shiver bird,

flying down south.

GLOW bird,  SNOW bird, north winds BLOW bird,

slide bird, ride bird,

berry bird, **merry** bird, weathering the storm.

rather be **inside** bird,

cuddle bird,

huddle bird,

feathers feel warm.

Tall bird,

Small bird,

isn't scared
at all bird,

scratch
bird,

hatch
bird,
peeping
from
an egg.

s i n k bird,

pink bird,

standing on one leg.

Glide bird, wide bird,

wading in the **tide** bird,

nod bird, **prod** bird, beak stuck in the sand.

Highland bird,

island bird, nesting in the rocks.

spire bird,

wire bird,

magic flaming fire bird,

bug bird,

snug bird,
living in a box.

Zzz

love bird, dove bird, give a gentle shove bird,

shriek bird, speak bird, big long beak bird,

HOW RUDE!

flap bird,

tap bird,
pecking
at a tree.

TAP
TAP
TAP

stunning
bird,

cunning
bird,

finding
a key.

Loon bird,

tune bird,

beak looks like a **spoon** bird,

big bird,

twig bird, building a nest.

TWeet bird, feet bird,

key bird,

street bird, meat bird,

free bird...

Did you spot Rare Bird?

PUFFIN BOOKS

UK | USA | Canada | Ireland | Australia
India | New Zealand | South Africa

Puffin Books is part of the Penguin Random House group of companies
whose addresses can be found at global.penguinrandomhouse.com.

www.penguin.co.uk   www.puffin.co.uk   www.ladybird.co.uk

Penguin
Random House
UK

First published 2021
001

Copyright © Michael Whaite, 2021
The moral right of the author has been asserted

Printed in China

The authorized representative in the EEA is Penguin Random House Ireland,
Morrison Chambers, 32 Nassau Street, Dublin D02 YH68

A CIP catalogue record for this book is available from the British Library

ISBN: 978–0–241–37891–5

All correspondence to:
Puffin Books, Penguin Random House Children's
One Embassy Gardens, 8 Viaduct Gardens, London SW11 7BW

for Merrick